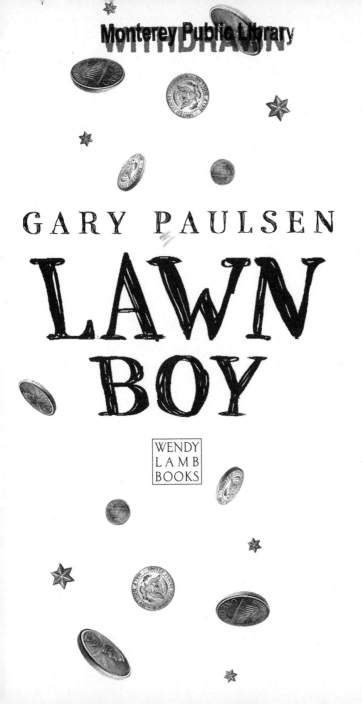

GARY PAULSEN

LAWN BOY

WENDY
LAMB
BOOKS

Published by Wendy Lamb Books
an imprint of Random House Children's Books
a division of Random House, Inc.
New York

WENDY LAMB BOOKS and colophon are trademarks
of Random House, Inc.

www.randomhouse.com/kids
Educators and librarians, for a variety of teaching tools,
visit us at www.randomhouse.com/teachers

Library of Congress Cataloging-in-Publication Data
Paulsen, Gary.
Lawn boy / Gary Paulsen. — 1st ed.
p. cm.
Summary: Things get out of hand for a twelve-year-old boy when
a neighbor convinces him to expand his summer lawn mowing business.
ISBN 978-0-385-74686-1 (trade) — ISBN 978-0-385-90923-5 (glb)
[1. Business enterprises—Fiction.   2. Summer
employment—Fiction.]   I. Title.
PZ7.P2843Las 2007
[Fic]—dc22
2006039731
Printed in the United States of America
10 9 8 7 6 5 4 3 2 1
First Edition

With all gratitude to Britten Walker

FOREWORD

I don't have a clue how all this will end.

There are people now who say I'm some kind of wonderboy or that I know some secret and that I had this big hairy plan.

Nope.

One minute I was twelve years old and wondering where I could get enough money for an inner tube for my old used ten-speed. I didn't have any money and my parents didn't have much either. My mom is a teacher in an experimental school and my dad's an inventor. Sometimes it takes a long time to work out a new idea. This was one of those times so we were a little bit broke. Mom and I have learned not to ask too many questions about what he's doing because if we do, he wants to use us as guinea pigs and we learned our lesson during what we now refer to as the Voice-Activated Door Incident. Dad swears Mom's nose is as cute as ever and I don't notice anything different about it, but she still touches it gingerly when he starts talking about some big new idea he's got going.

The next minute, it seems, I've got a business of my own, with employees, and I'm rich.

I'd better explain.

It all began at nine in the morning on my twelfth birthday when my grandmother gave me an old riding lawn mower.

1

The Principles of Economic Expansion

My grandmother is the kind of person who always thinks that no matter how bad things might seem, everything will always come out all right. Her hair could be on fire and she'd probably say, "Well, at least we have light to read by."

She's the most positive person in the world, and amazing and fun to be around, but in a strange and happy way sometimes she seems to be about nine bricks shy of a full load.

You can say, "You know, I think the Yankees will win the World Series again."

And she'll answer, "Yes, but it's still nice to put carrots in stew for the flavor."

And you think that somewhere inside that brain maybe a screw came loose. Then you find out that the last time the Yankees won the World Series she made a stew and forgot to put carrots in, and blamed the Yankees (she'd never liked them anyway) when the stew tasted funny. She still doesn't like the Yankees.

"It all makes sense if you wait long enough," she says.

So when I turned twelve she came to the house with an old riding mower in the back of her Toyota pickup.

"Happy birthday," she said. "It used to belong to your grandfather. He was always working on it. I thought you might like it."

"A mower?" Though we lived on the edge of what was termed an upper-middle-class neighborhood—Eden Prairie, Minnesota—our house was small, a "fixer-upper" when my folks bought it four years ago. It had a yard the size of a postage stamp and the grass never seemed to grow enough to need mowing. It just sprouted, stopped, gave up and died. Over and over.

My father and I lifted the mower down from the truck bed. "A lawn mower?" I looked at Grandma. "Thanks."

"My bridge club is meeting on Thursday night," she said, getting back into her truck, "which makes it hard to watch *CSI* since it's on Thursday too. Did you know that?"

And she drove away before I could answer her, much less wait for the part where it made sense.

"It appears you now have a lawn mower," my father said, smiling, as he walked back into the house. "I don't know the connection with her bridge club either, although I'm sure there is one. She's your mom's mother, maybe your mom will know what that meant."

I looked at the mower. Very old, low, small. It looked like it only cut about a two-foot-wide area, and it was nothing like the fancy new machines. The seat was steel, without a pad, and the driver's feet went over the top of the motor to rest on two foot pedals. One was a brake, the other a clutch that you had to push down to get the mower moving. It steered with two levers, like a very small bulldozer, and looked more like a toy than a mower.

Okay. Since I was twelve, I didn't have much

experience with motors. I've never even had a dirt bike or four-wheeler. I'm just not machine oriented.

My birthday present sat there. I tried pushing it toward our garage, but it didn't seem to want to move. Even turning around to put my back against it and push with my legs—which I thought might give me better leverage—didn't help; it still sat there.

So I studied it. On the left side of the motor was a small gas tank, and I unscrewed the top and looked in. Yep, gas. On top of the tank were two levers; the first was next to pictures of a rabbit and a turtle. Even though I'm not good with machines, I figured out that was the throttle and the pictures meant fast and slow. The other lever said ON-OFF. I pushed ON.

Nothing happened, of course. On the very top of the motor was a starting pull-rope. What the heck, why not? I gave it a jerk and the motor sputtered a little, popped once, then died. I pulled the rope again and the motor hesitated, popped, and then roared to life. I jumped back. No muffler.

Once when I was little, my grandmother, in her usual logic-defying fashion, answered my request for another cookie by saying that my grandfather had been a tinkerer. "He was always puttering with things, taking them apart, putting them back together. When he was around nothing ever broke. Nothing ever *dared* to break."

Loud as the mower was, it still wasn't moving and the blade wasn't going around. I stood looking down at it.

This strange thing happened.

It spoke to me.

Well, not really. I'm not one of those woo-woo people or a wack job. At least I don't think I was. Maybe I am now.

Anyway, there was some message that came from the mower through the air and into my brain. A kind of warm, or maybe a settled feeling. Like I was supposed to be there and so was the mower. The two of us.

Like it was a friend. So all right, I know how *that* sounds too: We'll sit under a tree and talk to each other. Read poems about mowing. Totally wack.

But the feeling was there.

Next I found myself sitting on the mower, my feet on the pedals. I moved the throttle to the rabbit position—it had been on turtle—and pushed the left pedal down, and the blade started whirring.

The mower seemed to give a happy leap forward off the sidewalk and I was mowing the lawn.

Or dirt. As I said, we didn't really have much of a lawn. Dust and bits of dead grass flew everywhere and until I figured out the steering, the mailbox, my mother's flowers near the front step and a small bush were in danger.

But in a few minutes I got control of the thing and I sheared off what little grass there was.

The front lawn didn't take long, but before I was done the next-door neighbor came to the fence, attracted by the dust cloud. He waved me over.

I stopped in front of him, pulled the throttle back and killed the engine. The sudden silence was almost deafening. I stood up away from the mower, my ears humming, so I could hear him.

"You mow lawns?" he asked. "How much?"

And that was how it started.

2

The Growth of Capitalism

When it all began, it was simple.

Our neighbor's house had a larger yard than ours, with what looked like good grass. No difficult corners, just a big square with a large elm tree in the center.

I mowed it, and he gave me money.

Twenty dollars.

Figuring that I used almost all the gas in the tank, about a gallon, which cost three dollars, and not counting the wear and tear on the mower (I didn't know how to figure that out), I made seventeen dollars for my work. It took two hours so I made eight dollars and fifty cents an hour.

That, I was to learn later, was called capitalism.

While I was finishing up that lawn the next neighbor up the block came by and said:

"How much to mow my lawn?"

Wow. Another job, just like that.

I poked around in our garage and found an old three-gallon gas can. I walked to the station on the corner, bought gas, brought it back, filled the tank and mowed the second guy's yard.

And while I was doing that a third man came and asked me to mow his lawn. The lawns kept getting bigger, and soon it was dinnertime and I had done three lawns and had made sixty dollars and I had a small piece of scrap paper with phone numbers and addresses for six *more* lawns. . . .

Turns out the man who owned the lawn service that had done all the yards in our neighborhood had run off with the wife of one of his customers and all the husbands were worried about hiring a new company after what had happened. A kid like me mowing their lawns wouldn't be much of a threat, I suppose. Plus, I was cheap.

Later I would learn that I had tapped into something called an expanding market economy.

All I knew was that it felt good to have all that money in my pockets.

That evening I took a rag and wiped the mower down, parked it in a corner of the garage and—a little admission here—patted it on the top of the gas tank. As I bent over, the wads of bills cracked in my pockets. Thanks, Grandpa. I never really knew my grandfather but the mower seemed tough and friendly. Maybe it was like him. He had worked on it and used it and it was nice to think of him as part of it.

Then I went inside. A strange thing happened.

My parents were getting food on the table and as we sat down to eat my dad said:

"That new film about astronomy is on at the IMAX. It would be great to see it." He sighed and I knew he was thinking about our budget.

And there I sat. My pockets full of money. And I could have said no problem, I've got money, and I'll earn more money tomorrow and more money the day after that. . . .

But I kept my mouth shut.

I could have said all those things but nothing came. Somehow it didn't feel right for me to be the one offering to take us all to the movies. If I did that, wouldn't Dad feel worse? Wouldn't it sound like I was bragging?

I ate my meat loaf and green beans and then went into the living room and watched a little television. Or tried to. I still had the sound of the mower in my ears so I couldn't hear the set. And my whole body was still vibrating from sitting on the mower all day. After a few minutes, I couldn't keep my eyes open. By eight o'clock I was sitting on the couch with my head hanging forward, drool dripping onto my T-shirt, sound asleep.

Mom shook me awake and sent me up to bed, where I crashed onto the pillow, still dressed, pockets full of bills. End of day one with my lawn mower.

And that was the easiest day.

3

The Law of Increasing Product Demand Versus Flat Production Capacity

There was a second then or a minute or maybe even a day when things could have remained sort of normal.

The next day I moved the mower farther into the richer part of the neighborhood, where the lawns began to get larger while my mower seemed to get smaller. Of course it didn't really, but that's how it felt. Soon it became obvious that I could only do three or maybe four lawns a day if I worked from just before dawn to just after dark.

And while it's true that the owners of the larger

yards paid me more—I was getting thirty to forty dollars a lawn the second day—there was also the distance factor. I had to ride the mower from lawn to lawn and as I moved farther from our house that meant it would take me longer to get home at night, putt-putting down the edge of the street on the mower. Plus, I had to stop every few hours to buy more gas, and that really chewed up my time even more than the bigger yards. Great mower, small tank.

I must have been the only kid my age in what felt like a ten-block radius who hadn't signed up for sleepaway summer camp or who wasn't on baseball and/or swim and/or tennis teams that summer— I was burned out on sports after spring baseball league. All the older guys had real jobs like at the Clucket Bucket or the Dairy Whip and all the guys my age were mostly busy or gone, so I had a long summer full of nothing ahead of me, almost as if I'd known how things were going to work out. Which, of course, I hadn't.

More and more people wanted their lawns mowed—on the second day I had eight jobs—and the fact was that I was fast approaching my limit.

Three lawns a day, plus refilling the tank from time to time, was all I could manage, and I would have to mow the lawns every week. Three lawns a day, once a week, twenty-one lawns if I worked seven days, dawn till dark, no days off.

Making approximately six hundred and thirty dollars a week.

It seemed like a staggering whop of money. Summer was twelve weeks long, which meant that by the end of vacation I would have made over seven thousand five hundred dollars.

Way, *way* more than I needed to buy a new inner tube for my old ten-speed.

And of course, there would be no vacation.

Which ran through my head as I worked. No vacation, no summer fun, no bike trips with my best friend, Allen, when he came to visit his father in the summer.

No vacation.

Seven thousand five hundred dollars.

No summer fun.

Seven *thousand* five hundred dollars.

I had just finished the second yard of the second day, and I was already a little sick of the sight of grass, grass, grass. The only sound in the world seemed to be the sound of the mower. The vibration of the seat was the only feeling my butt had ever known.

And then I met Arnold.

He showed up on the sidewalk when I started the third yard of the day.

Another customer, I thought.

I had plenty of time to study him as I mowed toward him.

Very short. I'm pretty short and he wasn't much taller than me and kind of round. Not fat, not heavy, just round. Everything about him was round. Rounded shoulders, hips, arms, legs—even his head was a ball. And his haircut looked like somebody had put a large bowl on his head and cut around it with scissors.

Wild clothes. I saw a seventies show on television once and everybody had shirts with impossibly long collars and colored patterns that looked like maybe somebody had taken a bucket of flowers dipped in paint and thrown it at the actors.

That was Arnold's style.

And he had a wide, wild tie and a kind of sport

16

coat that looked suede but was cut with wide lapels and shoulders and a narrow waist that didn't look too good on his round body. He looked like somebody who had flunked clown school. It was hard not to smile.

He waved as I approached and I stopped and pulled the throttle back to turtle. I liked that. Turtle or rabbit. Not written—not FAST or SLOW—just a picture of a turtle or a rabbit. Everything should be like that. Highway signs, posted signs in the hallways at school. Turtles or rabbits. It's so simple.

"I hear you're the new lawn boy."

I nodded.

He went on. "My name is Arnold, Arnold Howell, and I'm over there on the corner. How much would you charge for my lawn?"

I looked past him. It was good-sized, but flat and with not much detail work. "Would forty dollars be all right?"

"Thirty-five would be better."

"Well . . ." Other people had been paying me forty dollars for a lawn that big and that seemed fair. "I guess. . . ."

"The thing is, I'm having a cash-flow problem

and I'll have to scramble to find even thirty-five dollars. I'm a stockbroker and I work from home and I'm a bit overextended right now."

All of which was more than I needed or wanted to know. But he seemed okay and I thought he had an honest face—which turned out to be right, except that I'm not sure what a dishonest face would look like. Maybe a sneaky turtle? Or a shifty rabbit?

"Tell you what," he said. "How would you like to barter—take it out in trade?"

"I don't know what you mean." I didn't think he'd have anything I wanted. Not clothes. Especially not clothes.

"Like I said, I work out of my home. I do mostly day-trading. Work the small board, so to speak. I mean it's far-out, a real groovy way to work . . . and I make a nickel now and then, you know, moving this and that."

Was he crazy? Or one of those people with something loose in his brain? Somehow he forgot he was talking to a twelve-year-old kid with an old riding mower who knew nothing about the stock market.

"So, like, you're too young to have an account of your own but I could run the thirty-five dollars I owe you in on my account and make a purchase for

18

you. It would be in my name but you would get the proceeds. What do you think?"

"I don't know what you're talking about. You're going to buy something for me with money you owe me but don't have?"

"Exactly."

"What are you going to buy?"

"Stock."

"What's stock?"

"Shares in a company. You would buy shares in a company."

"Why?"

"Because then if the company does well the shares go up in value and you sell them to someone else and make money."

"That's how the stock market works? It's that simple?"

"Well, yes. With a whole bunch of rules and regulations and controls, that's pretty much how it works."

"And you always make money?"

He shook his head. "Not always. That's the . . . beauty of it. If the stock you buy goes down, you lose money."

"Oh."

"You have to be aware of that and buy carefully."

"Well then, the secret is to only buy stock that goes up."

Arnold nodded.

"How hard can it be?" I shrugged. I didn't have a clue what I was talking about. But it seemed pretty basic, and I had pockets full of money. I hadn't figured out where in the house to hide it where my mother couldn't find it, so I kept it jammed in my pockets.

Arnold made it all seem so easy.

"Let's do it," I said.

4

Capital Growth
Coupled with the Principles
of Production Expansion

I guess you'd say that I'm a pretty normal boy. Intelligence-wise.

I mean it's true that my parents are very smart people. Maybe not about money, but in other ways. My dad is full of ideas and how to tackle them. He even understands Einstein. My mother can do amazingly complicated math in her head.

I'm not like that. Now, I can read, and learn things; I go to a regular school in Eden Prairie, and I get good grades. Maybe *good* is too strong a word. I get all-right grades.

And with my average brain and average grades I lead a pretty average life. When I was small I played with toys, made models. I sometimes still make models. I went through a massive video game phase and still like to play now and then. I like girls but can't talk to them. Not a word. I try to be nice to everyone, and polite to old folks, people over twenty or thirty.

So there's nothing to explain what happened to me that summer. It's easy to say it was all just luck. But it's hard to believe there wasn't some kind of force behind it.

After meeting Arnold, I wasn't sure exactly what he was going to do, but two days later, I mowed his lawn and he told me that he would buy me not thirty-five dollars' worth of some kind of stock but forty dollars', which was the original amount that I'd wanted for mowing his lawn. "You're right," he said, "that's a fair price.

"I bought you stock in a small company that makes coffins. They're just starting up and the stock is going for fifty cents a share."

"Coffins? You mean for dead people?"

"Right."

"But I don't want any coffins."

"You're not going to get any. You're going to get eighty shares of stock in a company called the Memorial Wooden Container Corporation."

"Well, good. Because a coffin . . . that's more trouble than I need right now."

"Is something wrong?" We were standing on Arnold's front steps and he handed me some kind of hippie iced tea that tasted sweet but, he said, had no sugar in it. He studied my face.

"Nothing, really. It's just that I'm getting more and more jobs. I can't do them all and I have to start turning them down."

"Supply and demand." Arnold nodded. "It's groovy, man. The very nature of the concept of economic structure. You just need more mowers, more people, to meet the growing demand. The previous lawn service—before, of course, the unfortunate instance of the romantic . . . mishap—had a small crew of workers to handle the burden of all the lawns you're now working. You need to start distributing the wealth, dispersing the work. Far-out. It's beautiful."

"Well, it might be beautiful, but I can't do it. I don't know anybody—"

"I might"—he held up his hand—"be able to help you with this."

"Help me mow lawns?"

Even his smile looked round. "No. I'm busy. But I've done some investing for a man named Pasqual. He knows lots of people who are always looking for work. He's a good, reliable person, known him for years. Can you come back after dark?"

"Well, sure, I suppose. Not real late because my parents want me in by nine. But . . ." Alarm bells were ringing in my head. "Why only after dark?"

"Pasqual looks after his kids during the day. When his wife comes home from her job, then he goes to work."

"He mows lawns when people are sleeping?"

Arnold shook his head. "No. He does other work that isn't so noisy. Trimming, fertilizing—that sort of thing. Quiet things that won't wake the neighborhood."

"In the dark?"

"He wears a headlamp. Ingenious, really. I admire his creativity in the face of opposition. Entrepreneurship at its finest—there are no impossibilities, just hurdles to be overcome."

"Is it, you know, safe?" Kenny Halverson's uncle

said he didn't like half the things he saw in the day-light and that there was a very good reason for being afraid of the dark. If we were supposed to be out in the dark, Kenny Halverson's uncle said, we'd be born with night-vision goggles on our heads.

"Pasqual is honest, which is really what you wanted to know. And yes, he's safe. If you don't want to meet him, that's fine. Just keep your business at its present level. But if you want to expand, I think Pasqual can help you."

Five days earlier I had been wondering where I could find enough money for a bike inner tube and now I was considering how I could expand my business to distribute work and disperse wealth. I shook my head at how weird things had gotten and looked back at Arnold.

"Okay. Let's talk to Pasqual."

"Groovy. I'll call him right now. We'll meet him tonight."

And so we did.

5

Labor Acquisition and Its Effect on Capital Growth

"Hi," he said. "Arnold says you want to talk to me about work." Pasqual had the reddest hair I have ever seen in my life. My grandmother once told me, "You can always trust a redhead. They sometimes have mean tempers, to be sure, but they've usually got good hearts." Of course, we were at a baseball game at the time and I'd asked her to help me figure out my favorite player's batting average, but I still thought it was pretty good advice and so I liked Pasqual right away.

We were at Arnold's house. I had about twenty minutes before I had to be home. I had told my parents that I had to talk to people about new jobs and they'd extended my be-out time to nine-thirty.

"It's nice that you've found a way to make some spare change," Mom had said. "But aren't you working too hard?"

I'd jammed my hands in my pockets, pockets that were crammed with, at that moment, something like three hundred and thirty dollars, and said, "I like the work. It's good to be out in the fresh air." My parents are big on me spending time in the fresh air, for some reason. She'd smiled at me. "I'm so glad you're having such a good summer. I was a little worried things would be too quiet for you."

I decided to jump right into it with Pasqual since my time was short. "I have a lot of job offers I can't take because I'm working alone with only one mower. If I had help and maybe another mower . . ."

Pasqual nodded. "How many jobs do you have waiting?"

I thought. "I could probably have eight more. I don't really know how many might be coming along."

Another nod. "I understand. Tomorrow morning look for a small truck and a mower. A man named Louis will be driving. He's my . . . cousin.

Tell him which lawns to cut. I'll come when it's dark and do what silent work is needed."

"How . . . Who do I pay?"

"I receive half of what you get for the lawns that Louis and I do and I shall pay Louis out of that half."

"Half? I don't do anything and I get half?" I shook my head. "That doesn't seem fair. Shouldn't you get more?"

Pasqual smiled, his mustache turning up at the corners and then down. "You take half because you are the boss. You found these jobs, and will find more. That's the way it's done."

"But it's too much."

Arnold coughed. It was the first sound he'd made since we'd started talking. "It can be adjusted later if you still feel that way. For right now, let's just come to an agreement to get the process rolling."

I shrugged. "Fine with me. I guess."

Pasqual held out his hand and we shook.

"Louis and the truck will be here at Arnold's house in the morning. You leave the money with Arnold and he'll pay us."

And he was gone.

Arnold and I worked out new prices, since Pasqual would be doing additional work. We also figured out a smaller percentage for me. I stood there for another minute thinking.

"Is something wrong?" Arnold asked.

I shrugged. "I don't really know what to do. I've got all this money and I don't want to have it around the house where my parents could find it. . . ."

"Will they steal it from you?"

"Oh no, that's not it. I don't want to tell them about the money until the end of the summer."

"Why wait until then?"

"I'm waiting for the right time. So it doesn't sound like I'm kind of bragging or something."

Arnold rubbed the back of his head, then his face. "Tell you what: if you want, I'll keep it here, invest it for you, the way we did with that first stock the other day. That way your money will make money while you earn more."

I had a good feeling that Arnold was honest, and smart about investing, so I gave him most of the money, keeping just enough for gas for the mower. He gave me a receipt.

If I'd known what was coming I might have fired up the mower, stuck it in max-rabbit, and putt-putted all the way home to hide in my room.

6

Economic Expansion Combined with Portfolio Diversification

Two weeks passed.

Fourteen days passed, three hundred and thirty-six hours flew by, twenty thousand one hundred and sixty minutes whistled past, twelve million ninety six thousand seconds roared away. . . .

Numbers, all numbers.

And that's what happened to the time. It turned into numbers.

In the beginning, I had a routine.

I got up early, had some cereal before my parents even woke up, grabbed a gallon jug of water from the fridge and packed a bag lunch that I'd eat on the back of the mower while I was working (there was never any time to stop for lunch so I got good at eating and mowing), then left the house to start work. First, I checked the oil in the mower. Pasqual showed me how to do it and because it's an old engine, it needs a fair amount of oil. Then I added oil if I needed it, filled it with gas, and headed off down the street to Arnold's house.

Where I met Louis, a thin man with a small pickup. For two weeks, we loaded my mower on a small trailer he pulled behind the pickup and headed to our latest jobs. And at the end of the day we went back to Arnold's and I would ride my mower home and fall into bed until the next morning.

Louis and I were doing three lawns a day each with Pasqual coming to work in the evening and early morning to do edge work and cleanup. One night I stayed late to talk to Pasqual.

"We can't keep up," I said. "We're locked in to a ginormous number of lawns now, once a week, and I'm having to turn more people down."

"No." Pasqual shook his head. "Don't turn away work. Soon the summer will pass, the grass will be gone, and the work will fly away. We must make our

lives while the summer is here. I know someone—
Benny. He has a truck and he'll come tomorrow
morning. I have another cousin who can help me at
night and others, if you get more jobs. But you must
not turn work down."

And so I went on adding lawns. I kept track of
them in a little notebook. Then I bought a larger
one and wrote down the names, addresses and date
mowed, so there was some order. Then I got jobs to
do shrub trimming and pool cleanup and sidewalk
edging and garage cleaning, and there were more
and more people working away.

One morning I arrived at Arnold's, putt-putting
down the edge of the road on my grandfather's old
mower, and there were four pickups and twelve people waiting there for me and I thought, My, Pasqual
has a large family.

And it was only the last week in June.

But I really didn't think of much besides keeping
track of the new jobs in my notebook and recutting
the lawns that came due and collecting the money
and handing it over to Arnold. He put aside my percentage and gave the rest to Pasqual when he came
to work at night. Pasqual paid everyone else. Then

I'd ride home to dinner with my parents, sleep and head off to work on my mower again.

Once or twice Grandma came over for dinner. "I see you're making good use of that old mower. Which reminds me: Maggie Doyle and I are going to take a pottery class through the senior center this winter." She nodded happily and reached for the rolls. Even in my exhaustion, I noticed the glance my parents exchanged over the salad bowl. "But don't work too hard." Grandma smiled at me. "Is that grass in your hair?"

I had grass everywhere. In my socks, in my cereal bowl every morning, on my toothbrush. My shoes were stained green, I couldn't smell anything but fresh-cut grass, and I dreamed about endless lawns and enormous piles of clippings. I found myself thinking about how to best lean into turns so that the mower wouldn't leave rough patches that needed to be trimmed by hand. I spent a great deal of time wondering if I could rig an umbrella to the mower to keep the sun off my face, not because I minded the heat but because when I squinted, I made the rows uneven. I dug through old copies of *Sports Illustrated* to look for pictures of major-league ballparks' outfields so that I could study the patterns the grounds crews left behind in the nap of the grass.

But mostly the work cycle took over and I kind of missed the bigger picture.

Until one morning I putted to work and there were five pickups and more people all with mowers and bags and rakes. . . .

About then Arnold and I sat down and he said, "It's inefficient to have you all meet at my place every morning, and besides, the neighbors are starting to wonder why so many people congregate here."

So we decided to send everyone directly to their job sites from their homes and I'd go around with Louis in his truck and supervise and collect the money to bring back to Arnold, who would give Pasqual his share and put mine in my account that was in his name.

And it was then, that first time that Louis and I drove around, that I began to see that what was happening was bigger than just a few people running around mowing lawns.

7

Overutilization of Labor Compounded by Unpredicted Capital Growth

It was raining. This was the first day all summer it had rained hard enough to stop work. It was now July and I had ridden my ten-speed—yes, my old one, though I had bought a new inner tube—over to Arnold's house.

Arnold had made the hippie tea that was sweet without sugar and I sipped it while we dragged out the notebooks. I had left all the paperwork at his house because it would have been too hard to explain to my parents. There were now five three-ring binders. And in fact I knew almost nothing about it myself—it had all been a kind of blur.

"It's all just too, too groovy," Arnold said, putting his tea down. "Free-market industry and capitalism at their best. It's like watching a really good documentary about business. Far-out."

"I don't know what we're doing," I said. "Not a clue. Except that we're cutting a lot of grass and I'm not getting much sleep. And this morning my mother said she was forgetting what I look like."

"It's lucky we got a rain day." We were in Arnold's screened-in porch and he had spread the notebooks out on a large round picnic table. "It gives us a little time for you to catch up and see the beauty of what you're doing."

The rain was hammering down, almost deafening, and I found myself liking it. I used to hate rain in the summer because it ruined vacation time. Now I thought rain was beautiful.

"We'd better start with an overall view of the lawn-cutting phase of your operation."

Oh yes, I thought—let's start with that. Like I knew anything. Like I would have an operation with phases.

"Currently, you have fifteen employees."

I stared at him. "That can't be right."

He nodded, smiling. "Surprising, isn't it? Technically I guess Pasqual is more of a partner. And really, they are all partners in a way—they share the income from their work with you, the company head."

"Fifteen?"

He nodded again. "Now, the truth is they earn their living because you found them work, and that brings up a second consideration of this phase of your operation."

"Fifteen people work for me?" I wished he would quit talking about my "operation" and its "phases." It was starting to sound like General Motors or something.

"Yes. And that should lead you to consider your responsibility as a business head. You owe your employees that consideration."

"Well, sure. If there's fifteen people working for me I should consider them. But I don't know what you mean specifically."

"Well, think of this. They're seasonal workers. When the cutting is done they're no longer employed by you. A responsible employer should set aside some of his income, a percentage, to give them a bonus when the season ends to ease their transition into other forms of employment."

"I should? I mean, yes, I guess I should. How does that work?"

"Well, first let's look at your personal gross income from lawn cutting, shall we? It's really the only figure that counts for this aspect of your operation."

"Of course." Aspect, I thought. First phases. Now aspects. Of my operation. I'm twelve years old and I have aspects.

"Well, for reasons we'll cover later, taxes are going to take a hefty bite, and you have some small expenses—gas for your mower, oil, that sort of thing. I kept track of those items in this expense notebook. Then there's my fee. I'm taking five percent across the board, for this and the market work, just to simplify things, rather than work on a sliding scale. All right?"

Oh my, yes, I thought. Let's keep it simple. I felt like I was drowning in aspects and phases. "Good? I mean, I guess it is . . . good. Sure, good."

"So, before taxes, my percentage, and expenses, you grossed out at just over eight."

"Eight what?"

"Eight thousand dollars."

"Eight *thousand* dollars?"

"Yes. Of course, like I said, that's gross, and your net won't be anywhere near that. I think you should perhaps set aside a pretty good chunk for employee relief—perhaps twenty percent. At this stage. Naturally that will go up as they earn more. They'll appreciate it when the season ends."

I had this sudden memory of when I was nine years old. Back then I thought that someday I might be a professional basketball player. This in spite of the fact that I'm fairly short and can't make a basket to save my soul. But I thought when I was nine that if I just had the right ball, a true professional ball made by Spalding, I would/could be good enough to be a professional player when I grew up. The problem was that the ball was expensive. There was no way my parents could spend that kind of money on one measly basketball, and I couldn't find a way to get enough money on my own. So I wound up with a cheap ball and (I thought) no chance at a professional basketball career.

How many balls could I buy with eight thousand dollars? Eight *thousand* dollars. I was only three years older now than I had been then. True, it was a big three years. But after just three years I could afford all the Spalding basketballs I wanted.

I was rich.

Rich.

What a strange word that was; it didn't really mean anything in itself. *Rich.* Short for Richard? Why does *rich* mean having tons of money? How many Spalding balls could I buy, really, with eight *thousand* dollars? Say they're twenty dollars each to make it simple. Five balls for a hundred dollars. Fifty for a thousand dollars. Four hundred. I could buy four *hundred* Spalding basketballs. . . .

"What do you mean?" I suddenly remembered something Arnold had said. "You said something about this being a small amount of money. Is that what you said? I don't know what you're used to having, but I can't think of eight thousand dollars as a small amount."

"Everything," Arnold said, "is relative. Taken in the whole scheme of things, eight thousand dollars, though significant, is not all that large. If Bill Gates, who owns Microsoft, for instance, could hold all his wealth in his hands and he suddenly dropped it, just on the way to the ground it would make over forty thousand dollars in interest."

"Hunh?" I tried to picture that. "Look, I understand that I don't have as much as Bill Gates. Still, I'm very satisfied with what I have. I honestly don't know what I would do with more money than that."

"Seriously."

"Absolutely. It's more money than I could even think of having. It wasn't that long ago I was wondering where to get enough money to buy an inner tube for my ten-speed. Now I could buy a whole new bike. I could buy a bunch of them."

"Well then"—Arnold shrugged and sighed—"we have a bit of a problem."

8

Dramatic Economic Expansion: Its Causes and Effects

"Your problem," Arnold said, "is both simple and a bit complex. More tea?"

"No. I'm fine." Outside, the rain seemed to let up a bit, then came down harder. I could hear thunder way off somewhere. "What are you talking about?"

He took a sip of tea. "Man, I like this tea. It comes straight from India, you know. All the yogis drink it. I hear the Beatles used to drink it all the time."

"Arnold . . ."

"Oh. Well, let's go back to when all this started, all right?"

"You bet. Please."

"You remember that I had a cash-flow problem then and instead of paying you cash I started an account for you under my own name because you're too young to have an account."

"Yes."

"And we bought eighty shares of a coffin manufacturing firm for fifty cents a share."

I nodded. "I'm still with you."

"There's some risk, of course, with buying what they call penny stocks, which these were, but I thought with just forty dollars invested even if the company went belly-up the loss rate would not be unbearable."

"I'm still here."

"Well, the stock did not lose. After the second quarter of the year, it turned out the company had a great deal of land in northern Minnesota—upwards of two thousand acres of hardwoods—that they planned to use to make the coffins."

Another sip of tea. I waited.

"This had not been reported initially, but the land with the valuable hardwoods was free and clear

43

and belonged to the company; it was part of their net worth that nobody knew about, and when word got out the stock rose dramatically."

"How dramatically?"

"Normally I dislike these things because they give a wrong impression about the stock market. Ten, twelve percent a year is a good figure to think about making in the market. These explosions are very unpredictable and there is always an element of risk and one shouldn't plan on—"

"How big an explosion?"

"The first day it jumped to just over ten dollars and I thought of selling. Stock purchased at fifty cents and sold for ten dollars gives an excellent return. But the sudden surge caused a lot of interest and people started wanting to buy the stock and that drove the price up further, and still further, and I finally sold at a hundred dollars and ten cents a share. So your forty-dollar investment brought you just over eight thousand dollars, less my five percent commission."

"You mean I have eight thousand dollars on top of the *other* eight thousand?" I dumped them together in my head. Eight and eight is sixteen. Sixteen thousand dollars. Less commissions and those other things. Taxes. Less taxes. Sixteen thousand dollars.

"Well, not exactly. I assumed I had a rather free hand with your investment so I reinvested it and some of the other money you've been giving me, and frankly, I took a daring risk with one stock. I invested my own money at the same time and took the same risk."

"What did you invest it in?"

"It was one of those freak software things. Believe me, normally I wouldn't give it a second thought—they're just too big a gamble. But the quarterly earnings looked good, they had a new idea about nationwide Internet use, something to do with vastly improving the speed. A company called Walleye. I bought you three thousand shares at sixty cents a share."

"And we lost?"

"Oh my, no. The new Internet system they evolved swept the country and the stock jumped to ten dollars and split, which gave you six thousand shares at five, then went back up to ten dollars and split again, which gave you twelve thousand shares, which climbed back up to five-fifty a share, hung there and flattened out. So I sold when it went back down to four dollars."

He had, as they say, gone past my knowledge envelope about the stock market. "So you sold my three thousand shares for four dollars?"

"No, no." He shook his head. "It had split and then resplit—you had *twelve* thousand shares at four dollars a share. I must point out that this kind of growth is unprecedented."

The numbers were there. I knew they were, but they didn't register. It was just too much to understand, to believe.

I was twelve.

That morning my parents were having trouble deciding if they could afford a newer used car.

Five weeks earlier my grandmother had given me her old riding lawn mower and I'd started mowing lawns.

I was only twelve and Arnold had sold twelve thousand shares of Walleye for four dollars a share.

"Forty-eight thousand dollars? Is that right?"

"Well, less commission, of course."

"Of course. Sure. Right. Uh . . . let me get this straight. . . ."

"Sure. I know it's all kind of far-out."

"No, wait. You're telling me that I started with an old lawn mower and I now have . . . what do I have?"

"Well, from all of your stocks and bonds right now, over fifty thousand dollars. It's less because I took out my commission, but I will of course reinvest it."

"Of course."

"All in solid, safe blue-chip stocks and government bonds." He smiled. "Perhaps you'd better take a few deep breaths. . . . You seem to be weaving a bit."

"I have fifty thousand dollars?"

"And change, plus the eight thousand from mowing."

"And change?"

"You," he said, smiling, "have had a very groovy month . . ."

But I didn't hear him finish the sentence.

I had fainted.

9

Conflict Resolution and Its Effects on Economic Policy

When I came to, there was a damp paper towel over my face.

"I'm sorry," Arnold said. "I thought I eased into it but I guess the shock . . ."

I thought of a really important question.

"I . . ." I was still woozy. "I'm still not sure I heard you right. Did you say I now have over fifty thousand dollars?"

"Are you going to faint again?"

"No. I don't think so."

"Then yes. You are now worth that."

"Where is it?"

"In your account. Under my name, but in your special account."

"Can I see it?"

"Of course. I have your account information on the computer." He turned to his keyboard and tapped a few keys.

"No. The money. Can I see the money?"

He shook his head. "It's not like that. First you'd have to sell all your investments and get a check, then you'd have to take the check to the bank and cash it, and then, yes, you could see the money. And when you sell, you then owe taxes on your capital gains. At the end of the year, capital gains is what they call the profit you made from your initial investment."

"Oh." I didn't quite follow all that.

I thought.

"So I don't really have the money," I said slowly. "I have a computer screen and numbers and stocks and things . . . but not the actual money."

"That's right. That's how it works. You—or I, acting for you—will reinvest the money in safe stocks, which will give you what's called a diversified portfolio—so if one thing goes down another might go up—to cover you. But it's all there, and you can cash it in anytime you want. Except . . ."

"Except what?" I smelled a rat.

"Right now the money appears to be mine because legally you can't invest in the market because you're too young. You have to go through an adult. And I'm a little uncomfortable with this because first of all, I'm not your legal guardian, and second, since the money appears to be mine the government will want me to pay taxes on it and that shouldn't be my responsibility—to pay taxes on your money."

"So what do we do?

"Soon, very soon, we talk to your parents and get them involved."

Mom, I thought, Dad, I have something to tell you. I've been mowing lawns . . . I've been mowing a lot of lawns and I have fifty thousand . . .

Please pass the green beans and by the way I have fifty thousand . . .

Breakfast. Over toast.

Mom, Dad, you know how I've been mowing lawns every day? Well, guess what? I have—no, we have—something like fifty thousand . . . and change.

"There's something else."

What on earth could it be? How could anything in the world top this? "What is it?"

"As I said, I put your money into this Walleye stock, but I should remind you not *all* your money. I thought it might be good to do some investing for fun."

It isn't fun, I thought, to have over fifty thousand dollars?

"So there was this kind of fund for people interested in sports and I thought you might like to invest in that. . . ."

He trailed off and I studied him. "Is something wrong?"

He shook his head, looked out at the rain. I couldn't believe it was still raining, that it was the same day, that we had only been talking for an hour or so. Part of me was listening and part of me was imagining what the money would do to help my parents, what it would buy.

"I misread the explanation on the fund," he said, and sighed. "Usually, in this kind of fund, a lot of investors pool their money and perhaps buy a baseball team, or help to build a stadium. But it didn't turn out that way."

"How, exactly, did it turn out?"

"It turns out that you own one-hundred-percent interest in a heavyweight boxer who lives nearby."

"I *own* him?"

"Not really the person, of course. You're sponsoring him, and if he does well you split the purse."

"He has a purse? What kind of prizefighter carries a purse?"

"That's a figure of speech. The purse is the prize money. His winnings."

"What's his name?"

"Joseph," Arnold said. "Joseph Powdermilk, Jr. I have the specs in the computer and can run you a printout if you like."

"Sure. I'd like to know more about him."

"Good, because he's due here in about fifteen minutes. He called last night and wants to meet his sponsor and thank him." Arnold shook his head. "Look, I'm really sorry about this. If you lose I'll cover it, all right? And as for meeting him, well, he asked about his sponsor and without thinking I gave this address, so if you want you can leave right now and miss it."

I shook my head. "No. And if we lose on this it's not your fault. Five, six weeks ago I was sitting in my yard wondering about an inner tube. Now I'm a thousandaire. Or something. You think I'm going to complain?"

"Some would." He sighed. "Some have. What if we'd lost?"

"Then we would have lost forty dollars. That's what we started with, right? We lose the whole Walleye thing and all we've really lost is that, the original forty dollars."

"Well, that's a healthy way to look at it."

There was a sudden clatter in front of the house and an old station wagon rumbled to a stop.

It sat almost wheezing, then the driver's-side door opened and with a great deal of difficulty a man got out. I say man, but this person looked more like a living mountain than a man.

"I see it," Arnold said, "but I don't believe it. How did he get *in* the car?"

He was wearing a big sweatshirt and sweatpants and as he moved up the sidewalk to the door his step was amazingly light for someone his size. Almost like a *really* big cat.

Even though he could see us through the screen of the porch, he knocked on the screen door.

"Please," Arnold said. "Come in."

A quick motion, a sideslip, and he was in the door and standing in front of Arnold.

"I am Joseph Powdermilk and I would like to thank you for being my sponsor." He faced Arnold and held out his hand.

I have never heard such a voice. It sounded like thunder a long way off. Muted, but deep, rumbling.

"Sorry," Arnold said, "wrong sponsor." He pointed to me. "This is him."

He turned, a mountain turning. "I am Joseph Powdermilk and I would like to thank you for being my sponsor."

He held out a hand as big as a whole ham. I put my hand out—it disappeared completely in his—and we shook. His touch was gentle.

"It's nice to meet you," I said. "My name is—"

Just then Pasqual's truck streaked up behind Joseph Powdermilk's station wagon and came to a screeching halt. Pasqual came running up to the porch.

I knew it must be serious because it was daylight. Pasqual *never* came out in daylight.

"Come right away!"

I got up. "What's the matter?"

"His name is Rock. He has two . . . guys . . . with

him. He says we've got to pay him or he'll harm our workers. He plans to take over the business."

"What can *I* do?"

"Come! If Rock doesn't meet the boss he'll cause a lot of trouble. Come *now*."

I hadn't taken a step before I saw Joseph Powder-milk move with me.

"I'll help," he rumbled. "I'm good at this."

I was out the door. "Good at what?"

"Trouble."

10

Force of Arms and Its Application to Business

Pasqual, Joseph and I jammed into Pasqual's truck. Arnold had said he would follow in his car, but Joseph said, "You don't need to come. I'm sure it will be all right."

I sat in the middle of the front seat and Joseph sat on the right. Pasqual hadn't seen Joseph before but seemed to accept that he would be coming with us. He looked at Joseph once, briefly, when Joseph squeezed into the cab of the truck and the whole truck leaned so I thought it would tip over. But then we were on our way.

The house where Pasqual's relatives lived was more or less a big box, with a good yard because they worked on it when they had time off. There were four trucks parked in front under the huge elm trees that stood along the street.

The first three trucks I recognized. The fourth one was a red pickup angled into the curb, not parked parallel like the others. A man was sitting behind the wheel with the driver's-side window open and two men were leaning against the end of the truck. One of them was pretending to clean his fingernails with a knife. Several of Pasqual's family members were standing around by the door of the house. They seemed a little afraid, maybe, but mostly confused.

"The one in the truck is Rock," Pasqual said, stopping.

Joseph opened the door and slid out. The truck rose visibly when his weight was gone. He shrugged as if to loosen his shoulders, strode up to the driver's side of the red truck, reached in and grabbed Rock by the neck and pulled him out through the window. Then, holding Rock by the neck and crotch, Joseph power-drove him through the window into the truck headfirst.

This happened fast. The man with the knife was still cleaning his fingernails when Joseph moved around the front of the truck, grabbed the arm with the knife and shook the guy like a dog shaking a snake.

The knife flew through the air and Joseph picked this man up by the neck and the crotch and threw him into the third man, knocking him sprawling.

Then Joseph picked them up one at a time and speared one into the passenger side through the window and the other into the back of the truck. He went back to the driver's side and stood over Rock, who had tried to scramble around but still had one leg hanging out the window.

"Don't hurt the boy who's my sponsor," Joseph rumbled, "or any of these people who work with him. If you do, I'll know and I'll come and pinch your head. Do you understand?"

"You're crazy!" Rock said.

"All that matters is that you do not hurt my sponsor or any of the people who work with him and you do not ask them for money. If you do I'll know and come and pinch your head. Do you understand?"

"Yeah, yeah! But this isn't over!"

"That doesn't matter. Only what I said matters. Start your engine and drive away."

Rock scrabbled to get the key turned in the ignition, slapped the shift lever down and tore away with one leg still sticking out the window and the other two men with their legs hanging out the passenger side and the back of the truck.

Pasqual's relations started a slow applause and soft whistles as Joseph came back to our truck. It had happened so fast that Pasqual and I hadn't had time to get out.

Joseph moved his bulk back onto the seat and the springs creaked as he sat down.

"Maybe," I said, slowly, "we should have talked to them first. You know, before you . . . well, just maybe we should have talked."

"We did talk," Joseph said. "Before we came, they talked and asked for money. Then, after I put them in the truck, I talked. Then they drove away. That's the best way. First talk, then handle the problem, then watch them go away."

"I'll remember that," I said.

Joseph nodded. "Some things are hard to remember but this one is easy."

I nodded. "Still, maybe next time, if there is a next time, we could talk a little longer first."

"Maybe." He sighed. "Maybe not. Each time is different."

Pasqual drove off but I saw that he was looking at Joseph out of the corner of his eye and he said something under his breath.

"What?" I asked.

"He's a force of nature. . . ."

"It was something!"

"A big storm sweeping down to clean all things away."

"I think it was more like an earthquake. . . ." I trailed off, thinking. "Joseph, do you have a boxing name? Like a catchy title?"

"My name is Joseph Powdermilk, so I use that when I box."

"I think we need something with a little more excitement to it. How about if we call you Earthquake?"

"Earthquake?"

"Right. We'll call you Earthquake Powdermilk the next time you box. How does that sound?"

"It sounds like it's not my name."

"Oh. Well, okay. Sure."

"*Wait!*"

I jumped back from the percussion of his bellow.

"Joey Pow," he said.

"Pardon me?"

"Joey Pow," he said. "It's catchy *and* it's my name."

"Joey Pow." I looked over at Pasqual, who was smiling at Joey. "I like it."

And just like that, I was the sponsor of a boxer, I had security for the business, and my fighter had a cool nickname. I love it when things work out like that.

11

Business and the Art of Creative Misrepresentation

It was still raining softly that afternoon as I pedaled home from Arnold's, but the sun was coming out and I knew we'd be able to work the next day.

I'd told Arnold what happened with Rock. He nodded. "As you become more successful you'll attract more attention. Good *and* bad. It's a fact of business. It was good that Mr. Powdermilk showed up. With our unique situation, it might be difficult to call the authorities."

"Are we breaking the law?"

"Not at all, not at all. But it might be difficult to

explain how all this could happen without your parents knowing."

I watched as Joey Pow waved, got in his station wagon and drove away.

"I'm going to tell them. I'm just waiting for the right time."

"Soon. The right time should be soon."

I nodded. "Maybe tonight."

And just for the record, I tried.

Mom came home around four o'clock from her summer job, Dad came out of his lab in the basement, I helped in the kitchen and we had a proper sit-down meal.

After the meal Dad read the paper and I helped Mom with the dishes and then we went into the living room to watch television. Just after Dad put the paper down and Mom turned the set on there was a moment.

"Mom, Dad . . ."

They both looked at me.

"I've been mowing lawns. . . ."

Seemed lame.

Try again.

"I mean, I know how hard you work. . . ."

Still lame.

Hmmm. All right. Shoot the moon.

"Mom, Dad. If you could have anything you wanted, anything, what would it be?"

Mom looked at me. "Is this a game?"

"No. Seriously. Anything you wanted—what would it be?"

She frowned, thinking. "Well, I would hope that you have a happy and fulfilled life."

"I mean stuff. Is there any kind of stuff you want?" I looked at Dad. "Same for you—anything."

"I'd agree with your mother and hope that you had a good life."

I have a good life, I thought. And I have over fifty thousand dollars. "Thanks, both of you. But, hey, like I said, I mean stuff. For yourselves. Isn't there anything *you* would want?"

They looked at each other and shrugged.

"Not a thing," Mom said.

"Me either."

"Oh, come on. I mean, think about it, anything, no matter the cost."

There was a silence. Then my mom laughed. "Oh, *I* know what you're doing. You've saved up some money from your lawn-mowing business and you want to help out. Isn't that it?"

"Well, sort of."

"Ohhhh." She smiled that soft mother smile. "That's very sweet, dear, but we . . . Who on earth is that?"

She had been sitting facing the front window, which looks out across the lawn—which by this time, what with Pasqual's efforts, was starting to look pretty good. He'd been so horrified by the condition of what he called "the boss's lawn" that he'd come by to recondition it. The change was a complete mystery to my parents, who made jokes about the lawn fairies who work on the grass when everybody is asleep. My parents were spending a lot of time relaxing in the evenings after work, admiring their miraculous lawn.

My mother stood and walked to the window. "My goodness."

I looked and was stunned to see the old station wagon with Joey Pow sitting in the front seat, his head down, dozing.

"Look at the *size* of the man. Why, he barely fits in the car."

Dad stood and went to the window. "Hmmm . . . the car looks kind of beat-up. I wonder if he's all right?"

"He's all right, believe me." It slipped out before I could stop it.

"You know him?"

Think fast. But I couldn't figure out how to explain how I had come to own the prizefighter in front of our house without a whole lot of details and I also didn't want to lie to my folks. "Well, sort of. I know him from the lawn jobs I've been doing. He's a good guy. I'll go out and see what he's doing here."

I was out the door before they could say anything.

"Joey . . ."

"Yes."

"What are you doing here?"

"I thought I'd spend the night here to make sure Rock's people don't find you."

"Well, gosh! Thanks. A lot. But Rock doesn't know my name or where I live. . . . Speaking of that, how did you find me?"

"I followed you on your bicycle."

"Oh. Well, look, I don't need any help right now. But thanks again. Besides, shouldn't you be getting sleep for training? When's your next fight?"

"Six days. Next Saturday night. It's on the list they send sponsors."

"I left the list at Arnold's. Oh, Joey, my parents don't know . . . what I do at Arnold's, and that I'm sponsoring you. Not yet, that is. I'll tell them, of course, but I haven't gotten around to it yet. I can't figure out a good way to tell them how everything happened and they might not understand my involvement in, well, the fight game."

"Don't you want to be my sponsor?"

"Oh no, that's not it; I'm glad that . . . um, we're working together. Especially after today—and thank you again for that."

"No problem."

"Is your fight next Saturday on television?"

"I think so. Can't you come to the arena, though? The sponsor should watch the fight in person."

"It would be hard for me to get there. But I'll watch it on television. I really will. I'm rooting for you, Joey. I know you're gonna win; I just feel it. Now go home and get some rest and concentrate on your training. You only have six days to get ready."

"I still worry about Rock."

"I'll be fine. Really. And thanks for everything."

He looked at me.

"I'll be fine."

He nodded.

And as I watched him drive away, I really believed it.

12

Team Management in Times of Uncertainty

The next day started out normal.

Or as normal as anything had been this summer.

The rain had stopped and the grass dried. I rode my little mower over to Arnold's to check the notebooks to see where the jobs were. By now the whole thing pretty much took care of itself. Everybody knew where to go, what to do.

"Well." I sighed. "Another day . . ."

Arnold nodded. "It's a good crew—they know what to do. It's the best kind of business. Everybody is happy, everybody makes money and the lawns get good care. Speaking of knowing what to do—did you talk to your parents last night?"

"I tried, Arnold. I really did. But then Joey showed up and the opportunity was gone."

"Joey showed up? What do you mean?"

So I told him about Joey following me home and how difficult it became to talk to my parents about all the money things. "I couldn't see just how to break it to them by explaining that I 'own' a heavy-weight prizefighter, so I figured I would maybe wait until tonight. Or this afternoon. It's Monday and they both get off work today at noon."

Arnold nodded. "All right, then. But for sure today. I'm really getting uncomfortable about keeping secrets from them. And I want your parents to set up a proper account for you."

"Today. For sure."

"What are you going to do now?"

"The Beckwith lawn. I might as well take my mower over there. Keep my hand in."

I worked for two solid hours and only had half the lawn done before I needed to refuel. I'd started to put gas in the mower when I remembered my cell phone. Arnold had bought a bunch of phones and given one to each of the crews and to me so that we could keep in touch throughout the day. It bothered me that I had the thing in a belt holster while messing with gas after I'd seen something on television about how cell phones might spark and blow things up, so I took it out of the belt holster and was just setting it on the ground when it went off. I had it set on vibrate so I could feel it because with that old mower there was no way I could hear it. The vibration scared me so much I dropped it. I grabbed it. The call was from Arnold.

"Hi. What's up?"

"It might be best for you to head home right now." His voice sounded clipped and unnatural.

"What?"

"Home. It would be good for you to head home."

"You mean your place or my home?"

"Yes. Right. Head for home now. . . . *Unnhhh!*"

And then nothing.

I looked around, half expecting to see something that would explain what I'd just heard. Nothing, of course. I went over Arnold's words again, trying to remember. I dialed his number. It rang and rang.

"This is Arnold. Please leave a message."

I started to leave one, then decided not to. Something was very definitely wrong. He had said "head for home." I looked at my watch. Nobody would be there for an hour. Why head home? Why not go to his house? And why had he cut off so abruptly?

Rock.

It must have something to do with him, but Joey Pow had pretty much taken care of that. Maybe not. Maybe Rock had come back and followed some of the men to Arnold's house and figured out that Arnold kind of ran the show.

And then they came this morning.

And what?

I had to go see. But carefully. I parked the mower and ran the four long blocks to Arnold's. I stopped across the street in back of the Jamisons' hedge and studied Arnold's house.

His Toyota was there as usual. Things seemed normal. Nothing was moving on the porch or in any of the windows that I could see. I watched for what seemed like an hour but it was probably only fifteen minutes or so. I tried to slow my breathing down from the run over and I clenched my hands into fists to stop the shaking.

I finally decided to walk up to the house and check it out and had started to creep out of the hedge when I saw it. Behind the curtain on the living room window, a man's head appeared. Just for a second the curtain shifted and I saw him. I moved back behind the hedge.

Rock. Either him or his identical twin.

So.

Rock was there. Probably with some of his men. And they must have Arnold.

So.

Now what? They had Arnold and they wanted . . . what? They wanted money. More money than before. For sure. But what else? They wanted me? Wanted me to get the money?

With a jolt I realized there was nothing I could do. Pasqual turned his cell off during the day so he could sleep, and even if I could get to some of the sites and get the men they might not be able to help.

I could call the police! I had a cell. Three numbers. Nine-one-one.

But I didn't.

Would anyone believe me? A twelve-year-old kid calls the police and says he's running a huge business and somebody has taken over the house of his stockbroker?

No problem. We'll be right over. We just have to pick up the tooth fairy and Superman and we'll get right on it.

My heart sank even further when it hit me that I had no way to get in touch with Joey, either, who would have been my best ally. All the paperwork about him was still in Arnold's house. I didn't know his address or phone number or even where the fight was going to be on Saturday. Everything was in the house.

Where Rock was, either alone with Arnold or with more of his men.

I needed help. Now. I needed somebody smart who could think outside the box and help me figure out what to do about Rock and Arnold. Somebody with a good brain who would truly want to help me.

I needed my parents.

13

Expertise, Its Utilization and Effects on Economy

I ran the whole way home and saw the car in the driveway.

I burst into the house. They were in the kitchen with Grandma.

"Oh, hi, pumpkin," Mom said. "Would you like some lunch?"

On the run over I had decided I would tell them everything.

"Mom, Dad, Grandma, please sit down on the couch."

"How about lunch first?" Dad held up a knife covered with mayo.

"No time, no time. Please. Now."

Mom said, "You've been acting so strange lately."

"It's puberty," Grandma said. "He's becoming a man. Men act strange from time to time, and I am worried about what the hole in the ozone layer is doing to the plants in the rain forest."

"You know that guy who was sitting in the car yesterday?" I shook off the image Grandma had put in my mind and refocused on the situation at hand.

"The big guy?"

"Yeah, that's him. His name is Joseph Powder-milk. He's a professional boxer, a prizefighter. His next fight is Saturday night and if he wins I get half his winnings."

"What on earth are you talking about?" Mom asked.

"Why do you get half his earnings?" Dad frowned. "Why should he give you anything?"

"Because I bought his contract and I sponsor him."

They sat down.

"I mean, Arnold, my stockbroker, bought the contract for me.

"Arnold?" Dad asked.

"You have a stockbroker?" Mom whispered.

"His own boxer!" Grandma beamed.

So I told them the whole story. Fast.

They nodded, sometimes shook their heads, then nodded more. Listening, always listening, and I kept going, explaining Joey Pow and finally Rock and his gang. When I'd finished I took a deep breath. "And I think they're in Arnold's house now holding him prisoner. No, I *know* they're in there because I saw them and I don't know what to do."

Dad stood. "Call the police."

"At first I thought of that. But nobody would believe me anyway, even if I could call them."

"But with your parents with you, they would listen. . . . What do you mean at first and why couldn't you call them?"

"He means," my mother chimed in, "that it's difficult to go to the police because some of his employees are poor people who really need the money and if the authorities come into it, perhaps they'll find the workers aren't all documented the way they should be. Is that it, pumpkin?"

I nodded. "Thanks, Mom. I know we should call the police, but I was hoping there might be some other way—that you guys might be able to think up a way to solve this. . . ." I let it hang there. They were the smartest people I knew. If they couldn't come up with something nobody could.

Dad said, "We go to your strength."

"I don't think I have one."

"Sure you do! Literally. You know a prizefighter."

"But I don't know how to find him."

"Now," Mom said, "the thinking comes in."

It took her just three minutes on the Internet and two phone calls before I heard Joey's voice on the other end of the line. Meanwhile, I was shaking Grandma off because she wanted to say hello to him.

"Joey, it's me."

"The sponsor."

"Yes. Rock and his men are at Arnold's house, holding him prisoner, I think for money, and I can't call the police because a lot of the workers will get in trouble—"

I heard the phone click and Joey was gone before I finished speaking. I hung up and turned to my parents.

"Let's get over there."

"I call shotgun," Grandma said as we scrambled to the car.

14

Resource Utilization: Its Causes and Effects

At Arnold's we parked behind Joey's station wagon just as he was stepping out of the driver's side.

"Shouldn't we help in some way?" Mom asked, until she saw him standing. "On second thought, Joey can handle it. But we're going with him."

I got out of the car. No matter what happened, Arnold might need help either during or after. I started walking toward the house, Mom and Dad with me. Grandma brought up the rear.

I knew, or thought I knew, what was coming.

Joey had gone into the porch slowly, closing the

screen door quietly behind him. By that time we were close to the house. If the front door was locked it didn't slow him down. He hit it with his shoulder, took it off its hinges, and was out of sight.

There was a muffled, thumping sound. Oh no! Rock or his men might have a gun! Later I found it was just the sound of one of the men having his head jammed into a dishwasher. Without opening the door on the washer.

After the thumping, there was a second or two of silence, followed by a scream, and one of the men was thrown out the front door so hard he took the porch screen off its hinges and was propelled into the yard riding the screen on his hands and knees like it was a body board.

Until he hit the elm next to the walkway. The elm was probably a hundred years old, very big, and didn't give a millimeter when the man plowed into it facefirst.

A few seconds later, Joey came out with Rock in his right hand and another man in his left, carrying them like cats by the backs of their necks. The first man was still in the kitchen jammed into the dish-washer.

Later I found out that Rock and three others had

been in the kitchen with Arnold tied to a chair. They thought Arnold had told me to come to his place, and they'd been planning to force me to give them money when I came.

"I told you," Joey said, "to leave the sponsor alone or I would pinch your head."

"Please, Mr. Powdermilk." Mom was standing by the sidewalk, a half horrified, half admiring expression on her face. "Couldn't you just give them a stern talking-to?"

"Yes, but I did that before, when they made trouble the first time. I told them that I would pinch their heads if they came back. They came back anyway. Talking to them again won't help. Pinching their heads will."

Grandma was nodding.

"I won't come back," Rock said. "I promise this time. I really do. You don't have to pinch my head, really. I'll do what you say."

"See, Mr. Powdermilk?" Mom nodded. "I think he means it."

Joey stared at Rock in one hand, then studied the man in his other hand. He peered over at my father, who shrugged and said, "He seems to be telling the truth."

Then Joey turned to Grandma, who said, "Probably not the best move, young man, although personally, I'd like to see you pound the snot out of them."

Joey sighed and looked back at my mother. "If you really don't want me to . . ."

She shuddered. "I would really rather you didn't."

"All right. But if they come back, I'll have to take care of things my way."

"I understand. And *they* understand—don't you?"

Both men nodded enthusiastically.

"Then please let them go, Mr. Powdermilk," Mom said.

He dropped them and it was like watching those cartoon scenes where a dog or cat is held off the ground and his legs start moving faster and faster until he's dropped and he shoots away.

They disappeared in half a second.

We all went into the kitchen and found Arnold tied up but not gagged. I introduced him to my parents and Grandma while we untied him.

The man slumped against the dishwasher was regaining consciousness. Joey picked him up by the neck and threw him the length of the hallway and out the front door.

Arnold was none the worse for wear and made a pitcher of his special iced tea for us. We all had a glass while Arnold explained how he wanted to set up my account with Mom and Dad, and Grandma asked if Arnold could find her a boxer to sponsor too. Then my mother held her glass up and said, I think, a line from Shakespeare:

"All's well that ends well."

Except.

That wasn't the end.

15

Serendipitous Activity and Its Effects on Capital Quantity

We all went to the fight Saturday night.

It was a huge auditorium with a ring in the middle and a bunch of fat men smoking cigars that smelled like dog poop when a hot mower blade hits it. Women with not a lot of clothes on were hanging on to the men.

Because I was a sponsor, I had ringside seats for Arnold and my family, and when we arrived it was pretty exciting. Joey came out in a big red robe, followed by his manager in a red T-shirt. He took off the robe and pumped his arms in the air. He had on red trunks. The ring announcer introduced the fighters and we cheered like crazy. Grandma blew kisses, which made Joey blush and look away. The other man wore green. When the bell rang the fighters came out of their corners and took a stance in the middle like they were going to box.

Only they didn't.

The man in green swung at Joey and Joey ducked a little and used his right to hit the other guy so hard it sounded like somebody had slammed a melon with an ax.

The other boxer slid backward, already out cold, until he hit the ropes, then slithered between the bottom rope and the mat and out of the ring to land in the lap of a fat man smoking a cigar. We all jumped up screaming, "Joey! Joey! Joey Pow!" He waved a glove at us.

The fight lasted four and a half seconds.

That was it.

The purse was five thousand dollars and I was due for half. Wow. This was just the start for Joey; he was going to have many more fights. When I went to bed that night I had a dream about him doing a whole bunch of four-and-a-half-second fights until he became world champion.

It was a great dream, in color, with Joey wearing

the red trunks for luck and with a lot of action, and because it had been such a late night at the fight I slept hard. When the phone by my bed woke me up the next morning I was still in the dream.

"It's me," Arnold said. "We have a new development."

"Don't worry. . . . As long as he keeps wearing red trunks we're bound to win."

"What?"

The dream was hard to shake. "As long as he keeps wearing red trunks . . ."

"Wake up. It's me, Arnold!"

"Oh." I shook my head, scattered the dream. "All right. So what's the problem?"

"It's not a problem. You remember the Walleye stock?"

"Sure. The one that made me rich."

"That's the one. Well, I put in the sell order back when I said I did, and the records said it sold for four dollars a share and you came up with forty-eight thousand dollars . . ."

"And change."

"Yes. And change. Except the sell order didn't go through like the computers said it did and the stocks didn't change hands the way they're supposed

86

to. Some kind of technical foul-up. So for all of this week you have still owned Walleye stock. In fact, you still do. And there have been some massive shifts in the value—"

Even half awake I could feel a sinking in the center of my stomach. "How much," I said, though I didn't want to know, really, "did we lose?"

"Oh my. No. The stock didn't go down, it went up."

"Up?"

"Yes. There was a secondary merger of some stature and a larger software company took the whole thing over. They're always doing things like that, these high-risk software stocks. I remember when—"

"Arnold—how much?"

"Oh. Well, the merger triggered more interest, so the stock jumped to forty dollars a share. You have twelve thousand shares at forty dollars a share...."

Numbers.

More numbers. Twelve times four. Forty-eight. No, not forty-eight, but . . .

"Four hundred and eighty thousand dollars?"

"Yes. Of course, there will be fees and commissions and the like, but still, it should be just a little under that figure. Now listen, please. It's Sunday and the market is closed, but I heartily recommend that tomorrow morning when it opens we sell the stock and put the money in something solid and long-term."

I didn't faint.

This time I didn't faint.

But I did hang up and I got out of bed and went down into the kitchen, where Mom and Dad and Grandma were making a late breakfast, and without thinking about telling them to sit down I gave them Arnold's news and found there must be a weak male gene in our family because Dad fainted.

We put him on the couch.

"He's coming around." Grandma patted his hand. She turned to me. "You know, dear, Grandpa always said, take care of your tools and they'll take care of you."

ABOUT THE AUTHOR

Gary Paulsen is the distinguished author of many critically acclaimed books for young people, including three Newbery Honor books: *The Winter Room*, *Hatchet*, and *Dogsong*. His novel *The Haymeadow* received the Western Writers of America Golden Spur Award. Among his Random House books are *The Legend of Bass Reeves*; *The Amazing Life of Birds*; *The Time Hackers*; *Molly McGinty Has a Really Good Day*; *The Quilt* (a companion to *Alida's Song* and *The Cookcamp*); *The Glass Café*; *How Angel Peterson Got His Name*; *Guts: The True Stories Behind* Hatchet *and the Brian Books*; *The Beet Fields*; *Soldier's Heart*; *Brian's Return*, *Brian's Winter*, and *Brian's Hunt* (companions to *Hatchet*); *Father Water, Mother Woods*; and five books about Francis Tucket's adventures in the Old West. Gary Paulsen has also published fiction and nonfiction for adults, as well as picture books illustrated by his wife, the painter Ruth Wright Paulsen. Their most recent book is *Canoe Days*. The Paulsens live in New Mexico, in Alaska, and on the Pacific Ocean.